Gr 3.2

W9-BGA-221

P
Buller
   Felix and the 400 frogs.

MORRIS AREA PUBLIC LIBRARY
604 Liberty St.
Morris, IL  60450
(815) 942-6880

## A NOTE TO PARENTS

When your children are ready to "step into reading," giving them the right books is as crucial as giving them the right food to eat. **Step into Reading Books** present exciting stories and information reinforced with lively, colorful illustrations that make learning to read fun, satisfying, and worthwhile. They are priced so that acquiring an entire library of them is affordable. And they are beginning readers with a difference—they're written on five levels.

**Early Step into Reading Books** are designed for brand-new readers, with large type and only one or two lines of very simple text per page. **Step 1 Books** feature the same easy-to-read type as the Early Step into Reading Books, but with more words per page. **Step 2 Books** are both longer and slightly more difficult, while **Step 3 Books** introduce readers to paragraphs and fully developed plot lines. **Step 4 Books** offer exciting nonfiction for the increasingly independent reader.

The grade levels assigned to the five steps—preschool through kindergarten for the Early Books, preschool through grade 1 for Step 1, grades 1 through 3 for Step 2, grades 2 through 3 for Step 3, and grades 2 through 4 for Step 4—are intended only as guides. Some children move through all five steps very rapidly; others climb the steps over a period of several years. Either way, these books will help your child "step into reading" in style!

*For Felix Lawler Buchloh
and his 400 friends*

Copyright © 1996 by Jon Buller and Susan Schade. All rights reserved under International and Pan-American Copyright Conventions. Published in the United States by Random House, Inc., New York, and simultaneously in Canada by Random House of Canada Limited, Toronto. http://www.randomhouse.com/

*Library of Congress Cataloging-in-Publication Data*
Buller, Jon, 1943–
Felix and the four hundred frogs / by Jon Buller and Susan Schade.
p. cm. — (Step into reading. Step 3 book)
Summary: Felix, who has a gift for mental communication, is enlisted by the Frog Princess to help recover her magic moonstone from a mean neighbor's garden.
ISBN: 0-679-86745-7 (trade) — 0-679-96745-1 (lib. bdg.)
[1. Extrasensory perception—Fiction. 2. Frogs—Fiction. 3. Magic—Fiction.
4. Gardens—Fiction.] I. Schade, Susan. II. Title. III. Series.
PZ7.B9135Fe 1996 [Fic]—dc20 95-52061
Printed in the United States of America 10 9 8 7 6 5 4 3 2 1

STEP INTO READING

3 9957 00122 0215

Step into Reading™

# FELIX
## AND THE
## 400 FROGS

by Jon Buller and Susan Schade

**A Step 3 Book**

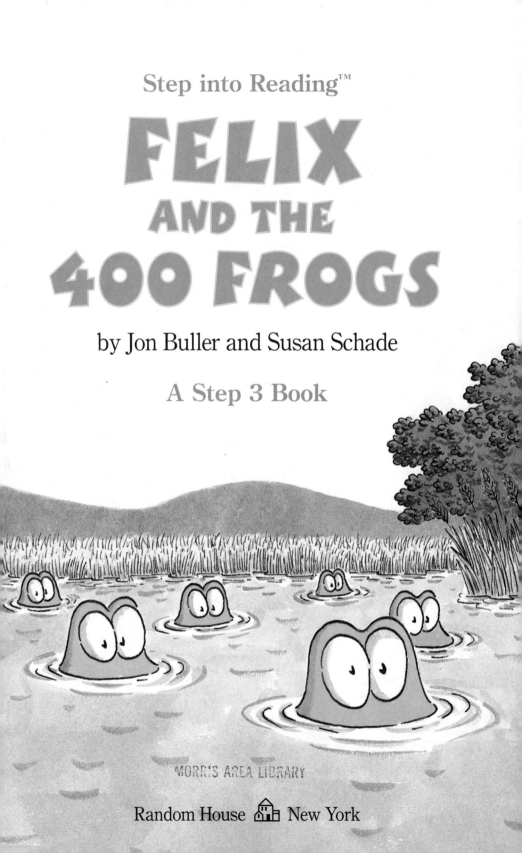

MORRIS AREA LIBRARY

Random House 🏠 New York

Felix was the last kid to leave the school on Career Day.

He had chosen his career!

He was not going to be a scientist, or a major league baseball player, or a bulldozer driver, or even a banker.

No, Felix was going to be something really different.

Felix was going to be a *mind reader!* Like Farina the Fabulous.

He walked home slowly. He was
remembering everything that Farina had
said.

He remembered how she had stared
into his eyes and said, "I can tell that you
have a gift for mental communication."

Felix stopped walking. He had a gift!

He didn't notice that he was standing
on his neighbor's sprinkler hose.

Mr. Nubble liked to keep his lawn nice. He was watering the grass with the sprinkler while he planted pansies in a perfect circle around his new lawn elf.

*Ffft*...went the sprinkler. *Ffft...ft*...And then it stopped totally.

Mr. Nubble frowned. All of his equipment was in perfect working condition.

Then he saw Felix, and his face flushed with anger.

"FELIX!" he yelled. "BONEHEAD! PEA BRAIN! YOU'RE STEPPING ON MY HOSE!"

Felix jumped off the hose. "Oh, sorry, Mr. Nubble. I guess I wasn't paying attention."

"Hoodlum! Airhead!" Mr. Nubble's voice level was approaching normal, but the veins in his forehead were still popping out.

Felix decided to send him a thought message. He stared into Mr. Nubble's eyes. *Felix is a nice boy,* he sent. *You like Felix.*

Felix could feel the thought waves pulsing out of his brain and radiating in Mr. Nubble's direction.

Mr. Nubble turned purple. "WIPE THAT LOOK OFF YOUR FACE WHEN I'M TALKING TO YOU!" he yelled. "NINCOMPOOP! RODENT!"

"I guess I need more practice," Felix
said to himself as he headed for home.

Felix decided to ride his bike down to the pond.

There was a big green frog sitting on a stump a few feet from shore. It seemed to be staring at Felix in a foolish way. Felix decided to practice thought waves on it.

He concentrated hard and stared into the frog's round eyes. *Come to me,* he sent.

*NO, YOU COME TO ME.* The words seemed to fill Felix's mind. They were so powerful he couldn't resist them.

He jumped.

SPLASH!

The next thing Felix knew, he was squatting in the water with his face six inches away from the frog.

"What happened?" he said to himself.

"You obeyed my mental command," said the frog out loud. "That's what happened."

"Wow," Felix whispered. "A talking frog!"

"I am not *a* talking frog," said the talking frog. "I am *the* Frog Princess. You may kiss my hand." And she held out a tiny webbed hand.

Felix took it carefully between two fingers. It was slimy. He was embarrassed, but he touched it with his lips.

Nothing happened. "Aren't you going to turn into a real princess?" he asked.

The Frog Princess snatched back her hand. "What do you mean?!" She was insulted. "I already *am* a real princess." A beautiful crown materialized on her head. "See?" she said.

"Wow!" Felix said again. "And you live in our pond?"

"What? In this mudhole? You have some funny ideas about princesses, Felix.

No, I live in the most beautiful palace in
the world—the Moon Lagoon!"

She sent Felix a mental picture of the
Moon Lagoon. He could see it in his head,
just like a photograph, all drooping moss
and sparkling pools.

"I am here on an important mission!" The Frog Princess told Felix. "This morning an evil red-headed man drove right up to the Moon Lagoon. He filled his truck with stones from the royal patio and drove away. And the worst of it is, one of those stones was *none other* than the MAGIC MOONSTONE!"

Felix was totally agog.

The Frog Princess continued, "We tracked the truck until we reached this town. I have brought my entire army!"

She waved toward the pond. Four hundred frogs' heads poked out of the water in unison. They gadunked loudly, "GA-DUNK! GA-DUNK! GA-DUNK!" It sounded like a twenty-one-gun salute. She waved again, and they sank back beneath the surface of the pond. Felix blinked.

"But now we have lost the trail!" the Princess wailed. "And we must find the Magic Moonstone before eight o'clock tonight!"

"Why?" asked Felix. "What happens then?"

The Princess gave him an how-dumb-can-you-get look and said, "That's when the *MOON* comes out. And if anyone is so much as touching the Moonstone, they will be flooded with incredible magic power! It could be a TOTAL DISASTER!"

"Cool!" said Felix. "Can I help?"

The Princess looked thoughtful.

"Can you move freely around the town without arousing suspicion or getting run over?"

"Of course!" said Felix. "I ride my bike."

"Then you shall be my driver!"

With one magnificent leap, she soared over Felix's head. "I'll ride here," she announced, settling on top of Felix's sweater in the basket.

"Don't tell anyone I'm not an ordinary frog." And her crown became invisible again.

Felix squished out of the pond and got on his bike.

"We are looking for a green truck," said the Princess, "or an evil red-headed man, or a plain gray stone that glows in the dark."

"That's not much help in broad daylight," Felix thought to himself.

"Precisely," said the Princess, making Felix jump. He had forgotten that she could read his thoughts. "And that reminds me," she added, "we will speak only through thought messages so no one will suspect who I am!"

Oh, boy! Felix would get a chance to practice.

They rode around the neighborhood.

Felix's first thought message was, *I see a green truck.*

*Wrong size*, the Princess sent back.

They saw four green trucks, six

redheads, and hundreds of gray stones,
but none of them pleased the Princess.

*Wrong, wrong, wrong,* she sent.

Then they rounded the corner by Mr.
Nubble's house.

Mr. Nubble was spraying a few scraggly dandelions with weed killer. The pansies were all planted around the new lawn elf.

"FELIX!" he yelled. "How many times have I told you not to ride your bike over my lawn when you go around this corner?!"

"I'm sorry, Mr. Nubble. I was in a hurry."

"LUNKHEAD!" steamed Mr. Nubble. His veins were bulging, and his face was getting red. "NITWIT! And what are you doing with that poor frog in your bike basket? You shouldn't mistreat animals, Felix!"

"I'm not mistreating her, Mr. Nubble. She likes it. Don't you, Prin...uhm, Froggie?"

The Princess nodded her head up and down and tried to look like a happy frog.

Mr. Nubble's jaw fell open, and Felix thought it would be a good time to leave.

"Bye, Mr. Nubble! I have to get home for supper."

MORRIS AREA LIBRARY

As soon as Mr. Nubble was out of sight, the Princess stood up and hissed, "That was him! That was the thief!"

"No, it wasn't," said Felix. "That was Mr. Nubble. He always acts like that. Besides, he doesn't have red hair. He's bald!"

The Princess hopped out of the basket.
"I didn't say red-haired. I said red-*headed!*"

She bounded off toward the pond. "Thanks for your help, Felix. We can handle it from here!"

Felix went home for supper.

After he ate, he had to wash the dishes, do his homework, and put on his pajamas.

Before climbing into bed, he went to his window and looked out. It was dark. He couldn't see much. But he could hear a lot of gadunking.

He looked over at Mr. Nubble's house. There was a small glowing light in the front yard. As Felix's eyes got used to the dark, he could see that it was coming from inside the new circle of pansies.

Felix remembered that Mr. Nubble always put smooth stones on the ground around his lawn elves so weeds wouldn't come up. That glow must be coming from one of those stones—the *Magic Moonstone!*

He ran down the stairs and out the back door.

"GA-DUNK! GA-DUNK! GA-DUNK!"
The frog army was lined up in rows on the
grass. The Princess was ready to launch
her attack on Mr. Nubble.

"WAIT!" cried Felix. "I know where the
stone is! Follow me!"

The Princess jumped lightly onto Felix's head.

He wheeled around, called out, "Forward…march!" and set off across the lawn. The four hundred frogs followed in perfect formation.

When they reached the neat round bushes that marked the beginning of Mr. Nubble's lawn, Felix put out his arms to stop the army.

There, at the foot of the lawn elf, was the glowing stone.

Felix beckoned, and the frogs began swarming silently over the grass.

But just then the edge of the moon rose above the trees, and the first ray of moonlight washed over the magic stone.

Felix gasped.

The stone, which was resting against the lawn elf's foot, turned into a ball of fire. The lawn elf stirred. It was coming to life! A horrible, evil grin spread across its face. It picked up the stone.

Then it went crazy.

FWOOOM! It flew around the yard like a balloon rocket.

"MA! HA! HA!" it laughed. It snatched up Mr. Nubble's pruning shears and threw them at one of the shrubs. They began cutting by themselves. CLIP CLIP CLIP.

They clipped the shrub into the shape of a horrible monster. And kept on clipping.

The boxwood became a *Tyrannosaurus rex*. The privet became two sinister sea serpents. "MA! HA! HA!"

ZOT! ZOT! Lightning bolts shot out of the elf's fingertips and turned the tops of the pillars into gargoyles.

ZOT! Another lightning bolt split the ground, and a thick brambly hedge grew up all around the yard.

The frog soldiers were hopping
frantically this way and that. But they
couldn't keep up with the magic lawn
elf.

The Princess moaned and cried, "Too
late, too late!"

Felix knew he needed to do something fast. And suddenly he had an idea.

Mr. Nubble kept a shiny ball on a pedestal. He called it a gazing globe, and it was about the size of a basketball. Felix ran over to the globe, grabbed it, and threw it to the elf, shouting, "Think fast, Elf!"

The elf whirled around, dropped the Magic Moonstone, and reached out with both hands to catch the globe.

The globe lodged between the two outstretched hands and stuck there.

The elf never moved again. All the magic had left him the moment the moonstone rolled away.

It rolled right into the waiting arms of the Princess.

The frog army cheered.

Felix bowed.

Then he heard the slam of Mr. Nubble's screen door.

Uh-oh.

Mr. Nubble's yard was unrecognizable.

It had been turned into a garden of horrible monsters. Besides which, it was full of frogs.

And Felix was right in the middle of them.

Mr. Nubble's face turned red, then purple. The veins in his neck bulged. His mouth opened and closed but only gurgling sounds came out. He was speechless.

Felix didn't know what to do. He looked around wildly for the Princess, but she seemed to have disappeared. And the frog soldiers were hopping back toward the pond.

Mr. Nubble started toward Felix.

Felix panicked. "HELP!" he thought.

*Don't worry, Felix.* It was a thought message from the Frog Princess! *I will now repay you for all your help. Go home and go to bed. I will take care of the red-headed Mr. Nubble.*

Felix was glad to escape alive.

Just before he slipped through the bramble hedge, Felix looked back. Mr. Nubble was staring at a small light that floated before him. The Frog Princess was using the Magic Moonstone on Mr. Nubble. Maybe, Felix thought, she was erasing his memory or something.

Felix yawned and went home.

Felix woke up in his own bed. It was morning. What a weird dream!

He made a piece of peanut butter toast and went outside in his pajamas.

Mr. Nubble's yard was hidden by a bramble hedge! Felix had *not* been dreaming!

There was a sign wired onto the bramble hedge. It read NUBBLE'S GARDEN OF MONSTERS, admission $1.00. Felix slipped in to have a look.

Mr. Nubble was trimming one of the monster shrubs.

"FELIX!" he yelled. "SNEAK! TIGHTWAD! Just because you live next door doesn't mean you can get in for free!

And what are you doing outside in your
pajamas?"

Felix smiled and went home to get
dressed. Mr. Nubble hadn't changed
at all.

Later he went down to the pond and threw pebbles at the lily pads. He would miss the Frog Princess.

*She was a little too stuck-up for my taste.* The thought message entered Felix's mind.

He looked around. There was nobody there but an old snapping turtle on a log. And it was staring into Felix's eyes.